My adventure to Umrah

Rahima Islam

Chapter one

I'm going on an adventure, I'm going to *Umrah*.

"What is *Umrah*?" I hear you ask.

Umrah is a journey to the House of *Allah* (SWT), the Holy *Kaaba* in the Sacred Land of Makkah in Saudi Arabia.

Wow, that's sounds amazing!

Sometimes people call *Umrah* the mini-*Hajj* or the minor pilgrimage as it involves some of the rituals or traditions of *Hajj*.

I'll take you on a journey to *Hajj* another time, *In-Sha-Allah*.

Makkah was the place where the Prophets Adam (AS), Ibrahim (AS), Musa (AS) and Younus (AS) visited, it is the birthplace of the Prophet Muhammad (SAW), and it is the place where Prophet Isa (AS) will visit when he returns to the world.

The word *'Umrah'* means *'visiting a place,'* so I'm going to be a visitor. I'm going to visit the House of *Allah* (SWT), the *Kaaba*.

I'm super excited and can't wait to get there. I've packed my bags and I'm ready to go.

Come and join me as I take you on the journey of *Umrah* with me.

4

The *Kaaba* is not where *Allah* (SWT) lives, but it is considered the House of *Allah* (SWT) and I will be *Allah's* guest.

I feel special that *Allah* (SWT) has invited me to His house. I promise I will be a good guest and I'm going there to worship Him.

There are different ways to worship *Allah* (SWT) and performing *Umrah* is one of them.

Allah (SWT) said in the *Qur'an*,

"The very first house placed on earth for my worship was the Kaaba."

Why am I going to do *Umrah*?

Because *Allah* (SWT) said it pleases Him, He said in the *Qur'an*,

"Accomplish Hajj and Umrah to please Allah."

Umrah will also allow me to connect with *Allah* (SWT) and receive his blessings, mercy, and forgiveness, and it also cleanses my sins and purifies my mind, body, and soul.

The Prophet Muhammad (SAW) believed that *Umrah* is the best way to worship *Allah* (SWT) and seek His blessings and forgiveness.

The Prophet Muhammad (SAW) said,

"Worship at the Kaaba is 100,000 times better than worshipping anywhere else on the planet."

I feel blessed that I will get the chance to gain so much reward.

I'm going to travel to Makkah in an aeroplane, I'm going to fly across oceans to get to my destination.

Before I leave my house, I must purify myself and make the intention to *Allah* (SWT) for *Umrah*.

To purify myself, I'm going to perform *Wudhu*, I'm going to clip my nails and get in the state of *Ihram*.

"What is *Ihram*?" you ask.

Well, *'Ihram'* is the state of staying in purity, wearing certain clothes, and staying away from certain things which are normally *halal*.

I'm going to have a bath, wear my special clothes and read two *rak'ah salah*, then make my intentions.

I will say the following words for my intention,

"O Allah! I intend to perform Umrah. Make it easy for me and accept it from me."

Men must wear two sheets of white cloth, they must cover their chest and legs, but they aren't allowed to cover their ankles or head.

Women can wear anything modest, by covering their whole body including their hair, except for their face and hands.

Often the special clothes we wear for *Ihram* are also called 'The *Ihram*.'

We will stop any bad behaviours such as arguing, fighting, gossiping, and killing creatures and we will stop using perfumes, so no more scented soaps, shampoos, or lotions.

We could make the intentions at home, or we could make it at the *Miqat*.

"*Miqat*? so many new words," you say.

Miqat is the boundaries outside the Sacred Mosque where the *Kaaba* is located.

Once we have made our intentions, we are going to recite the *Talbiyah*, until we get to the Holy *Mosque*.

The *Talbiyah* are specific words we can say in our minds or out loud, as the ones below,

"Here I am O Allah (in response to Your call), here I am. Here I am. You have no partner, here I am. Verily all praise, grace and power belong to You. You have no partners."

I will stop reciting the *Talbiyah* when I see the *Kaaba*.

When I see the *Kaaba*, I know I am going to be in awe. I'm so excited, I just can't wait.

The *Kaaba* is a cube shape building draped in a black and golden threaded cloth located in the centre of the world.

There's something amazing about it, that words just can't explain. I think you have to see it to understand what I'm talking about.

Chapter two

Let me tell you about how the *Kaaba* was built.

It is believed that the Holy *Kaaba* was first built by the Prophet Adam (AS) with the commandment of *Allah* (SWT).

It was used as a place of worship, but over the years, people stopped worshipping *Allah* (SWT) and the *Kaaba* was destroyed.

Then *Allah* (SWT) commanded Prophet Ibrahim (AS) and his son Prophet Ismael (AS) to rebuild it.

Between the time Prophets Ibrahim (AS) and Ismael (AS) died and the Prophet Muhammad (SAW) was born, many people tried to destroy the *Kaaba*.

The King Abraha of Yemen, who came from Abyssinia was jealous of the number of people that visited the *Kaaba*, he built a Church and wanted people to come to his

Church and when they didn't, he came to attack the *Kaaba* with his elephants.

Allah (SWT) protected the *Kaaba*, by killing him and his elephants with the help of birds who attacked the enemies with hardened clay.

This story is mentioned in *Surah Fil* in the *Qur'an*.

The *Kaaba* started to be filled with idols and people began to worship idols instead of *Allah* (SWT).

Idols were made from stone and shaped in the form of people. People did many terrible things around the *Kaaba*.

The *Kaaba* was destroyed by a flood and was then rebuilt at the time of the Prophet Muhammad (SAW).

The leaders of Makkah were enormously proud of their new building, but they argued about who should place the Black stone in its place. They all wanted to feel important.

Chapter three

"What is the Black stone and where did it come from?" you ask.

Some people believe that the Black stone, also known as *Hajar-al Aswad* was given to the Prophet Adam (AS) when he was sent to earth.

Others believe that the Black stone was given to the Prophet Ibrahim (AS) from

Jannah, it was delivered by the Angel Jibreel (AS).

The Black stone was originally pure white, but over time with the sins of people and the touching and kissing, it has turned black.

The Black stone was even stolen from its place but was later returned.

The leaders of Makkah decided, whoever enters the *Mosque* next, should decide who would put the stone back in its place.

The Prophet Muhammad (SAW) entered the *Mosque* and helped them solve their conflict.

He told them to place the Black stone on a sheet and for all the leaders to hold the corners of the sheet and he gently placed the Black stone in its place.

All the leaders were happy with that decision because they all felt important.

The Prophet Muhammad (SAW) wasn't happy that the *Kaaba* was being used to worship idols, he wanted it to be used to worship *Allah* (SWT) again.

After many years, *Allah* (SWT) fulfilled his dream, and the *Muslims* were able to use the *Kaaba* for worshipping *Allah* (SWT) again. They destroyed all the idols and only allowed *Muslims* to visit it.

Chapter four

I'm therefore going to Makkah to worship *Allah* (SWT) in front of the *Kaaba* and around it. I'm going to do *Tawaf.*

"*Tawaf?* What is *Tawaf?*" you ask.

Tawaf is when we are going to circulate the *Kaaba* seven times like the Prophet Muhammad (SAW) did when he performed *Umrah* and each time we circulate it, we will make lots of *duas*.

We will start at the corner where the Black stone is and we will read the following *dua*,

"Bismillahi, Allahu Akbar."

("In the name of Allah, Allah is the Greatest.")

We will go anticlockwise and every time we reach the Black stone, we will read the same *dua* and try to touch it and kiss it, because that's what the Prophet Muhammad (SAW) did.

However, hearing about the crowds that form there, I'm not sure I can get there, so what I might need to do, is point to it as I walk past it. I'll get the same rewards.

The thoughts of the crowds do scare me, but I'm going to hold onto my mum and dad's hands tightly, so I don't get lost.

During the first three rounds of *Tawaf*, men will need to walk fast or jog between the *Al Rukn al Yamani* corner of the *Kaaba* to the Black stone corner and there's a story why they do that.

One day while the Prophet Muhammad (SAW) lived in Madina, he had a dream that he was performing *Umrah*. He believed it was a sign from *Allah* (SWT).

So, he went with 2000 companions, including women and children to Makkah to perform the very first *Umrah* in the history of *Islam*.

The *Umrah* lasted three days and was one of the four *Umrah's* the Prophet Muhammad (SAW) performed in his lifetime.

When they got to Makkah, they became ill, they had a fever and felt weak, their enemies mocked them and laughed at them.

"The weak people have come with fever, and they are affected by evil."

They laughed at them from the top of mountains and surrounding areas.

Allah (SWT) told the Prophet Muhammad (SAW) and all the men to jog in the first three rounds when they were in the view of their enemies, so they jogged between the two corners.

Allah (SWT) also told the Prophet Muhammad (SAW) and the men to expose their right shoulder during the *Tawaf* to show their strong arm.

When the enemies saw the strength of the believers, they said,

"They are stronger and sturdier than us."

During *Tawaf,* men still jog in the first three rounds and expose their right shoulder to remember what the Prophet Muhammad (SAW) did.

While doing the *Tawaf,* there will be a semi-circular small wall near the *Kaaba* called the *Hateem*, I need to go around that too, I mustn't enter it while I am doing my *Tawaf.*

The *Hateem* is also known as *Hijr Ismael.* It is believed that the Prophet Ibrahim (AS) built this shelter for baby Ismail and his wife Hajar (RA).

I will try my best to touch the *Kaaba* and if I can't touch the Black stone, I'll at least try to touch the *Al Rukn al Yamani*, or even the door or the walls of the *Kaaba.*

Al *Rukn al Yamani* is just a corner of the *Kaaba* that faces Yemen.

If I get close to the *Kaaba* or if I can touch it, I know I will smell the scent of perfumes (*Attar*) which is sprinkled on the black cloth of the *Kaaba*.

I will make lots of *duas* as I go around the *Kaaba*, making *dua* for myself, my parents, my family, my friends and the *Muslim Ummah*.

As I walk from the *Al Rukn al Yamani* to the Black stone, I will do a specific *dua*,

"Rabbana atina fid dunya hasanatan wa fil akhirati hasantan wa qina azaban nar."

("O Allah! Give me good in this world, good in the hereafter and save me from the hellfire.")

When we circulate the *Kaaba*, there will be angels above us circulating another house up in the seventh Heaven called *Al Bayt al Ma'mur*.

Now that's something amazing to think about.

I think it's also amazing to think about how many people have visited the *Kaaba*, rich and poor, from all across the world at different times in history and the vast number of *dua's* that have been said here and even answered by *Allah* (SWT).

I hope all my *duas* are answered here too.

I have been trying to memorise some of the *duas* from the *Qur'an* and I have been trying to learn what these *duas* mean too.

Chapter five

There is a huge footprint engraved on a large stone, caged in a golden structure called the Station of Ibrahim (*Maqamil Ibrahim*).

Some people say that the Prophet Ibrahim (AS) used the stone to reach the top of the *Kaaba* as he built it, and others say he stood on it to call people to prayer.

The stone was softened for Prophet Ibrahim (AS) by *Allah* (SWT) and as he stood on it, his footprint was engraved on it.

I've been told the size of the footprint is like that of a giant, I wish I get to see it.

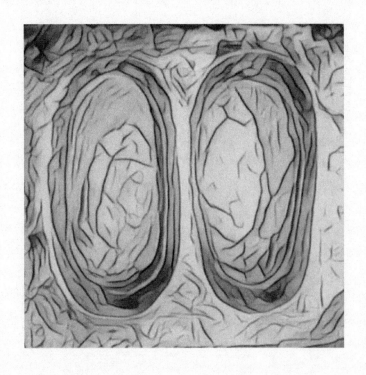

After I complete my *Tawaf*, I'm going to pray two *rak'at salah* behind the *Makamil Ibrahim*. Men must now cover their shoulders while performing *salah*.

It is recommended I recite *Surah Kafiroon* in the first *rak'ah* and *Surah Ikhlas* in the second *rak'ah* after *Surah Fatiha*.

I know these *surahs* by heart, so that shouldn't be a problem.

Chapter six

Then we will go to the taps of *Zam zam* and drink some water.

It is recommended that I face the *Kaaba* to drink the *Zam zam* water, starting with,

Bismillah (In the name of Allah),

then making *dua*, sipping it three times and finishing with,

Alhamdulillah (All praise is for Allah).

I'm going to drink as much as I can, and I can even pour some over my head.

Zam zam water is so blessed, so I'm going to try and get lots of blessings.

Then we will head to the two mountains, Mount Safa, and Mount Marwa, where we will perform *Sa'eey*.

"What is *Sa'eey*?" you ask me.

In Arabic, *Sa'eey* means to 'walk' or 'move quickly' and is a ritual where you travel from Mount Safa to Mount Marwah seven times.

So let me now tell you the story behind *Zam zam* water and *Sa'eey*.

The Prophet Ibrahim (AS) was commanded by *Allah* (SWT) to leave his wife Hajar (RA) and baby son Ismael in the barren desert.

This place was later to become the holiest place, *Masjid al Haram,* the *Kaaba*.

Prophet Ibrahim (AS) left his young family with some dates and some water in the middle of nowhere and as he turned around to leave, Hajar (RA) cried out,

"Oh Ibrahim, has Allah (SWT) commanded you to do this?"

Ibrahim (AS) replied,

"Yes."

To which Hajar (RA) said,

"If that is the case, then *Allah* (SWT) will not let us down."

Hajar (RA) had strong faith that *Allah* (SWT) would not abandon her and her baby.

As Ibrahim (AS) left his family in the desert, he made a *dua* to *Allah* (SWT) and this is mentioned in the *Qur'an*.

"Our Lord, I have settled some of my descendants in an uncultivated valley near Your sacred House, our Lord, that they may establish prayer. So, make hearts among the people incline toward them and provide for them from the fruits that they might be grateful."

Later, this *dua* was accepted from Ibrahim (AS).

When the dates and water had run out, Hajar (RA) and Ismael became extremely hungry and thirsty.

Baby Ismael cried out loud, but there was nobody around to hear his cry except his mother.

In desperation, Hajar (RA) searched for help. She ran from Mount Safa to Mount Marwa.

She stood on the top of the two mountains to get a better view of the area and to see if she could find any desert travellers to help her, she did this seven times

When she would not see anyone, she pleaded to *Allah* (SWT) to send her relief.

The mountains became the symbol of Hajar (RA)'s struggle and it is recommended to read the following *dua* when on the mountains,

"Innas safaa wal marwata min sha'aa'ir-illaah."

(Indeed, as Safa and al Marwa are among the symbols of Allah.)

From Mount Safa to Mount Marwa is one round; you must complete seven rounds.

Between Mount Safa and Mount Marwa, Hajar (RA) heard the cry of her baby and ran frantically to get to him.

To symbolise her struggles, the Prophet Muhammad (SAW) was told to run at an area between Mount Safa and Mount Marwa where there are now two pillars of green, fluorescent lights.

In the days of the Prophet Muhammad (SAW) the area of the two pillars were dipped like a ditch and *Allah* (SWT) told the Prophet Muhammad (SAW) to run in that area, to show his enemies his strength and speed.

It is therefore recommended for men to run in that area during *Sa'eey*, between the two pillars, but women do not need to run here.

The path in *Sa'eey* is no longer the sandy soiled floor it used to be, it is now paved, and the two mountains are protected by a coating.

Hundreds of thousands of people do *Sa'eey* each year, so the mountains need to be protected from wear and tear.

Sa'eey is no longer outdoors, in the hot and desert conditions, it's all inside a building now.

Although we may not get the same experience as Hajar (RA), we can still think about her struggles.

Then from a distance, where Hajar (RA) had left her baby, she saw a gush of water coming up from the ground.

She couldn't believe her eyes, she thought she was imagining it, but when she came running to her son, she was shocked to see a spring of water.

Angel Jibreel (AS) had come to help and with the tip of his wing, he hit the ground beneath baby Ismael's feet and out came the spring of water.

Subhan Allah! That's utterly amazing!

Hajar (RA) was overjoyed to see the water and she tried to scoop it up, she tried to make a well in the ground to collect the water, but the water continued to flow.

When Hajar (RA) could not stop the flow of the water, she called out '*Zam zam*,' which means 'Stop' and this is where the name of the spring came from.

The spring of water attracted travellers to stop and take a drink and over time, people started to settle there. The first tribe to settle there were the Jurhum.

Ibrahim (AS)'s *dua* had been granted.

The water continues to flow, we will be lucky to get to drink from it and although it's no longer a spring, it is available in taps.

After the *Sa'eey*, men will shave all their hair and women will cut a fingertip length. This symbolises the detachment from the world and allows everyone to come out of the state of *Ihram*.

That completes our *Umrah*.

Alhamdulillah!

Chapter seven

The strict rules will be lifted, and we will continue our *Umrah* journey by praying in the Holy *Mosque*.

Everything must be done in order without making any mistakes, but if I do make a mistake, I will have to do certain things to make up for it.

I may need to give *Sadaqah* (charity) or give *Damm* (sacrifice an animal) depending on my mistakes.

I must therefore be incredibly careful in following the rules while I am in a state of *Ihram*.

Although *Umrah* is a *sunnah*, which means it was done by the Prophet Muhammad (SAW), it is not compulsory like *Hajj*.

Hajj is a pillar of *Islam* and must be fulfilled by all abled *Muslims*.

I'll take you on a journey to *Hajj* next time, *In-Sha-Allah*.

I can do *Umrah* anytime of the year, except during the days of *Hajj*.

If I perform *Umrah* during *Ramadan*, I will get the reward equal to that of performing *Hajj*.

That would be awesome!

Allah (SWT) says in the *Qur'an*,

"We made the house a place of return for people and a place of security."

I want to return again and again in safety to the House of *Allah* (SWT), *In-Sha-Allah*.

We will then visit Madina, the land of the Prophet Muhammad (SAW) and pray in his *Mosque* and we may even do *Ziyarah*.

Ziyarah is visiting different places where the Prophet Muhammad (SAW) went, we may visit other *Mosques*, cemeteries, and important mountains.

Some people visit Madina and do *Ziyarah* first and then come to Makkah. It doesn't matter which way round you do it.

<u>Glossary</u>

Al Bayt al Ma'mur	The flourishing house in Heaven
Alhamdulillah	All praise is for Allah
Allah	God
Al- Rukn al Yamani	The Yemeni corner
AS	(Alayhi wa salam) - God be pleased with him
Attar	Perfume
Bismillah	In the name of Allah
Damm	Sacrifice of animal
Dua's	Prayers
Hajar al Aswad	Black stone
Hajj	Pilgrimage to Makkah
Halal	Permissible
Hateem/Hijr Ismael	Low wall of Kaaba

Ihram	State of purity/ Special clothes
In-Sha-Allah	If Allah wills
Islam	Religion of Muslims
Jannah	Paradise
Kaaba	House of Allah in Holy Mosque
Madina	City in Saudi Arabia
Makkah	City in Saudi Arabia
Maqamil Ibrahim	Stone with Prophet Ibrahim(AS)'s footprint
Masjid al Haram	The Great Mosque of Makkah
Miqat	Boundary to enter state of Ihram
Mosque	Place of worship for Muslims
Muslims	A follower of the religion of Islam
Qur'an	The holy book for Muslims
RA	(Radi Allahu anhuma) – May Allah be pleased with her

Rakah/ Rakat	Units/ unit of Salah
Ramadan	Month iin Islam
Sadaqah	Charity
Sa'eey	Ritual of walking or running between Mount Safa and Mount Marwa
Salah	Prayer
Saudi Arabia	Country in the Middle East
SAW	(Salalahi wa salam) – May the peace and blessing of Allah be upon him
Subhan Allah	Glory be to Allah
Sunnah	Traditions of the Prophet Muhammad (SAW)
Surah	Verse
SWT	(Subhanahu wa ta'al) - The Most Glorified, the Most High
Talbiyah	A prayer recited by Pilgrims

Tawaf	The circumambulation or circulation of the Kaaba
Ummah	Nation
Umrah	A visit to the Holy Kaaba
Wudhu	Abulation or ritual washing
Zam zam	Blessed water
Ziyarah	Visit to monumentous sites in Saudi Arabia

Photography and editing by Rahima Islam

Printed in Great Britain
by Amazon